UP, UP, UP!
IT'S APPLE-PICKING TIME

Jonathan

Golden
Delicious

Winesap

Gravenstein

McIntosh

Red Delicious

Winter
Banana

Granny Smith

Fuji

Red-Gold

Anna

Red Astrachan

Yellow Pippin

Winter
Pearmain

MacDonald

Arkansas Black

Stark Red

Pink Delicious

Beverly Hills

Newtown
Pippin

Rome Beauty

UP, UP, UP! IT'S APPLE-PICKING TIME

by
Jody Fickes Shapiro

illustrated by
Kitty Harvill

Holiday House / New York

For all the Fickes kids—
Gene's, Jim's, and Don's
—J. F. S.

To Darcy
—K. H.

ACKNOWLEDGMENT

A special thank you to Jim and Mary Fickes, for the years
of hospitality in See Canyon. They were the inspiration for this story.
J. F. S.

Library of Congress Cataloging-in-Publication Data
Shapiro, Jody Fickes.
Up, up, up!: it's apple-picking time / by Jody Shapiro; illustrated by Kitty Harvill.—1st ed.
p. cm.
Summary: Myles and his family go to his grandparents' apple ranch,
where they have a wonderful time picking and selling apples together.
ISBN 0-8234-1610-0 (hardcover)
[1. Apples—Fiction. 2. Grandparents—Fiction.] I. Harvill, Kitty, ill. II. Title.
PZ7.S52956 Up 2003
[E]—dc21   2002191318
ISBN-13: 978-0-8234-1610-3 (hardcover)
ISBN-13: 978-0-8234-2166-4 (paperback)

"UP, up, up!

It's apple-picking time."
Mama's voice tickles my ear,
whispers me awake.

On with my shirt, sweater, pants,
warm socks, and shoes not tied.

Outside it feels as if we're the only ones
awake in the whole world.
Dad says, "It's a long drive ahead."

Amber uses my shoulder for her pillow.
But I don't mind. She's keeping me warm
while we're driving, driving,
driving to the apple ranch.

Two picnics later—
one for breakfast, one for lunch—
we're finally off the highway and
onto the twisting, bumpy,
narrow bridge (one car only)
apple tree-lined road.

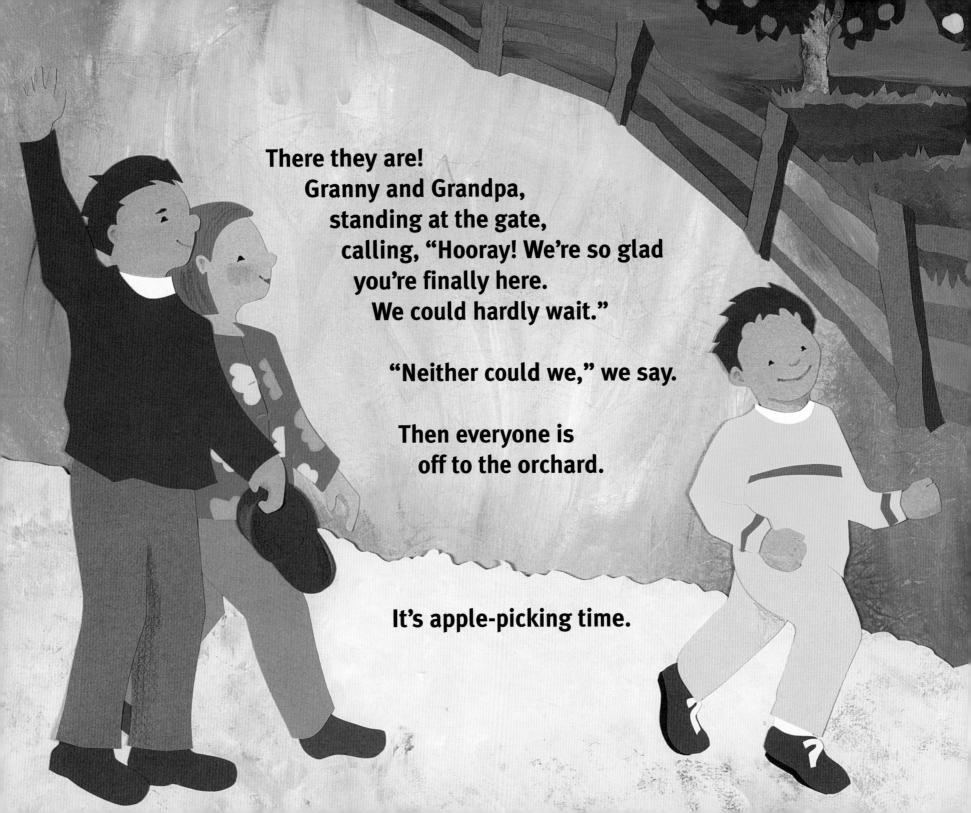

There they are!
Granny and Grandpa,
standing at the gate,
calling, "Hooray! We're so glad
you're finally here.
We could hardly wait."

"Neither could we," we say.

Then everyone is
off to the orchard.

It's apple-picking time.

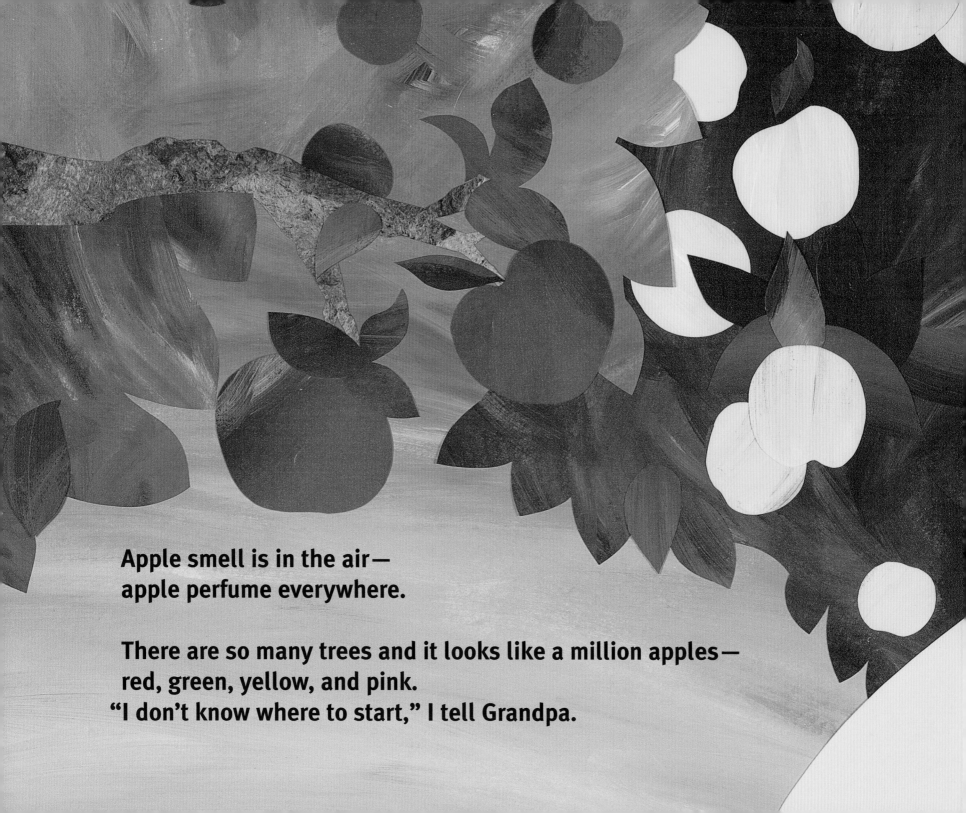

Apple smell is in the air—
apple perfume everywhere.

There are so many trees and it looks like a million apples—
red, green, yellow, and pink.
"I don't know where to start," I tell Grandpa.

He pulls a yellow apple off a tree,
puts it up to his nose, and breathes in
like Mama does with a flower.
"Ah, it's perfect apple aroma," says Grandpa,
and we lean in close and smell it too.

From his pocket he takes out his red-handled knife and cuts a slice out of the apple.

"Have a taste," he says.

The apple is cool and crunchy and sweet.
Everyone has a slice, and we all stand together
in the afternoon sunshine, wishing we could have more.

But it's apple-picking time.

"Begin with this
Golden Delicious, Myles,"
Grandpa tells me. He points
to the tree where we're standing and
hands me a small sack made from cloth.

I give the littlest tug and the yellow fruit almost falls into my hand. It's as big as my softball.

The sack gets
heavy fast.
Every time it's full,
I empty it into a
wooden field box.

We climb up ladders and disappear into the trees.
I can see Dad's legs. His voice is coming
from the middle of a tree filled with red apples.
He's singing a made-up song about loving
apple dumplings and eating apple pie.

The tree next to him has Mama's laugh.
That's the only way I can tell she's in it.

Amber and Granny are picking up fruit from the ground.
Granny says these apples make the best cider.

The mention of cider makes me want some.
It's warm work, picking apples.
I say that it already smells as if cider is hiding
somewhere in the orchard.

"That's apple-orchard perfume
you're smelling, Myles," says Granny.
Then she surprises us with cups of cool apple juice.

All afternoon we fill those apple sacks with Delicious—both red and golden—McIntosh, Pippin, Winter Banana (a funny name for an apple, if you ask me), and the last few stray Gravensteins.

The wagon cart is loaded with boxes filled to the brim.

Daylight runs out fast in that canyon, even in summer.

Granny's Pippin pie makes a fine end to an apple-picking day.

Early to bed. Have to be well rested for an apple-selling day.

"Up, up, up! It's apple-selling time." Grandpa's whiskers scratch
my cheek, and the smell of breakfast cooking pulls me out of bed.

It's Grandpa's morning oatmeal with sweet applesauce.
Then we're out to the fruit stand through the dew-wet grass.

Grandpa turns over
the carved wooden sign.
Cars pull in.

Granny, wearing a big straw hat trimmed
all around with shiny apples, greets old friends.
"These are the grandkids come to help."
She almost sings the words.

Apples are tasted, admired, and bought.

We carry bags and boxes of apples to cars for the people who come and go all morning. Lunch is a picnic in the sunshine, but we can hardly sit still enough to eat.

It's apple-selling time.

And then before you can say "McIntosh-Granny Smith-Golden Delicious-Pippin pie," the sun has flown away, taking the warmth with it. The sign is turned to "Closed." It's time to call it a day.

Supper is fresh-baked apple dumplings,
floating like islands in a sea of milk.
Then there's talking about that apple-selling day.

Grandpa puts old jazz records on his phonograph and dances around with Amber. Even Mama and Dad dance, but I like lying on the rug in front of the fireplace, just watching everyone being happy, wishing we didn't have to go home tomorrow.

It's hard to say good-bye— hello hugs are so much nicer.

Sackfuls of apples surround Amber and me. We're driving,
driving, driving home. Their cidery smell helps me remember
the happy days of apple-picking–apple-selling time.

GRANNY'S MICROWAVE-BAKED APPLES

Equipment: an apple corer (A carrot peeler will work too.)
measuring spoons and a measuring cup
a microwavable bowl (glass or china)
some waxed paper
a microwave oven
a hot pad

Ingredients: one medium-sized apple per serving
Choose any apple variety that is good for cooking (Golden Delicious,
Granny Smith, Gravenstein, Pippin, Rome Beauty).
$1^1/_2$ tsp brown sugar
$^1/_4$ tsp cinnamon
2 pecan halves broken into pieces (optional)
$^1/_2$ cup milk or 1 scoop vanilla ice cream

1. Have an adult, with the corer, carve a hole in the center of the top of the apple about halfway through the middle of the apple. Make the hole about as deep as your pinkie finger and as wide as your ring and pinkie fingers together.
2. Mix together the brown sugar, cinammon, and pecan pieces (if desired).
3. Put half of the mixture inside the hole in the apple.
4. Place the apple in a small microwavable bowl and cover the bowl loosely with waxed paper.
5. Microwave the apple on high for $1^1/_2$ minutes.
6. Let it cool for 5 minutes. Remove the bowl. (Make sure you use a hot pad or have an adult help you. The bowl will be hot.)
7. Take off the waxed paper and spoon the remaining sugar-cinnamon mixture into the center of the apple.
8. Return the bowl to the microwave uncovered for 25 seconds.
9. Let it cool for 5 minutes. Remove the bowl. (Remember! Use a hot pad or have an adult help you.)
10. Serve the apple with $^1/_2$ cup of milk poured in the bowl or a scoop of vanilla ice cream.

Jonathan

Golden
Delicious

Winesap

Gravenstein

McIntosh

Red Delicious

Winter
Banana

Granny Smith

Fuji

Red-Gold

JODY FICKES SHAPIRO makes regular visits to her family's California apple ranch and loves to pick, sell, and eat apples. She is the owner of Adventures for Kids, a bookstore for children in Ventura, California, where she lives.

KITTY HARVILL has illustrated several picture books for children. Her artwork has also appeared in a line of note cards and prints. She munches apples near Little Rock, Arkansas, in the company of her cats and parrot.